PLAYING THE GAME

First edition for the United States, Canada,
and the Philippines published 1991
by Barron's Educational Series, Inc.

Design David West Children's Book Design

All inquiries should be addressed to:
Barron's Educational Series, Inc.
250 Wireless Boulevard
Hauppauge, NY 11788

International Standard Book No. 0-8120-4659-5

Library of Congress Catalog Card No. 91-13501

Library of Congress Cataloging-in Publication Data

Petty, Kate.
    Playing the game / Kate Petty : illustrations by Charlotte Firmin.
       p.   cm. -- (Playgrounds)
    Summary: A young boy learns why games, even made-up ones, need
rules to make them fair.
    ISBN 0-8120-4659-5
    (1. Games--Fiction. 2. Fairness--Fiction. 3. Conduct of life-
Fiction.) I. Firmin, Charlotte, ill. II. Title. III. Series:
Petty, Kate. Playgrounds.
PZ7.P44814Pl   1991
(E)--dc20   91-13501   CIP   AC

Printed in Belgium
  34   98765432

PLAYGROUNDS

PLAYING THE GAME

Kate Petty and Charlotte Firmin

Barron's

Joel is watching his favorite cartoon on TV.
The good guys are tough.
When they fight the bad guys
the good guys always win.

Joel is playing his favorite computer game.
Whoosh. *Whoosh*. He likes to knock
his enemies down.

In the playground Joel plays
the tough guy. He kicks
the other children in fun.
It makes them angry but Joel laughs.

Then someone kicks him back.

It hurts and Joel cries.

"That's not fair," he says,

"I was only playing."

Joel joins in a game of tag.

Ahmet catches him in less than a minute.

"That's not fair," says Joel.

Alex stops to tie his shoelace.

"Truce," he says.

Joel tags him anyway.

"You can't do that," the others tell him.

Joel goes off in a huff.

He watches a group playing hopscotch.
"Let me play," says Joel.
But he jumps all wrong.

"You can't do that," says Chris.
"That's against the rules."
"That's not fair," says Joel,
and walks away.

Joel overhears another group
of children talking. They are
playing Mommies and Daddies.
"You're the baby," says one.
"You're not allowed to say anything –
just cry."

"And you're the dad," says another,
"So you're not allowed in the house
with dirty shoes on...."

"Rules, rules," thinks Joel.
"Every game has stupid rules."

But Joel likes to play soccer
during gym period.
He changes, quick as a flash,

and dribbles the ball
up and down the field.

He keeps an eagle eye on everyone else
to make sure they don't do anything wrong.
"Foul," he cries. "He can't do that.
That's against the rules."

Miss Smith looks surprised.
"I'm glad you pointed that out,
Joel," she says. "I was beginning
to think you didn't understand
the meaning of rules."

"But you have to have rules in soccer
or all the players could do anything
they liked. Then it wouldn't be a game."
"Exactly," says Miss Smith.
"And it's the same with every game."

During library period the librarian
helps Joel find a book on karate.
He looks at a book about soccer, too.

At home Joel watches TV.
Even the big football players
have all sorts of rules to learn.
Karate fighters do, too.

Joel is beginning to understand
why rules are needed — even for
made-up games. Everybody enjoys
playing more if they know that
the game is fair.

The next day Miss Smith asks Joel
to referee the soccer match.
He blows his whistle hard
every time he sees someone
breaking the rules.

Well, not every time...
Some people are just too young
to understand.

THINGS TO DO...

Draw a picture of Joel in the playground.
Or draw a picture of children playing games
in your playground.

Talk about the things Joel likes to do.
Talk about why the other children don't want
Joel to join in their games.
Or talk about the rules in your playgound.
Are there any other times when you need rules?

Make up a game and think up some rules for it.

Remember that rules help everyone to work
and play together. Some rules, especially
safety rules and the rules for sports, are
very important. Other rules can be made up
by you and your friends to make your games
fair and fun for everyone.

PRINTED IN BELGIUM BY

proost

INTERNATIONAL BOOK PRODUCTION